Published in the United States by Random House Children's Books,
a division of Random House, Inc., 1745 Broadway, New York, NY 10019.

Random House and colophon are registered trademarks of Random House, Inc.

Visit us on the Web! www.randomhouse.com/kids

Educators and librarians, for a variety of teaching tools, visit us at www.randomhouse.com/teachers

www.uglydollbooks.com

Library of Congress Control Number: 2008922395
ISBN: 978-0-375-84507-9

MANUFACTURED IN CHINA
10 9 8 7 6 5 4 3 2 1
First Edition

CHiLLY CHiLLY ICE-BAT

ICE

by David Horvath and Sun-Min Kim

Random House 🏠 New York

Welcome to Uglytown.
In Uglytown, summers are hot, hot, hot!

Especially in the tiny apartment of best friends Wage and Babo.

Wage and Babo's old, run-down air conditioner had not worked in many years.

"I don't think I can take this anymore!" moaned Wage.

"Let's give the air conditioner one last try," groaned Babo.

They tried hammering it.

They tried kicking it.

They tried taking it apart . . .

. . . and putting it back together again.
"All this work has made me even hotter!" said Wage.

Wage and Babo decided it was high time for a new air conditioner.

On the way to the store, Wage and Babo met Jeero and Tray. They were hot, too.

"We're going to buy an air conditioner!" Wage told them.

"Good times!" said Jeero sluggishly. "Please invite us over when you've turned your place into a winter wonderland," he joked.

Tray was too hot to speak.

When Wage and Babo arrived at Air Conditioner Kingdom, they were met by sneaky shop owners Ox and Wedgehead.

"We need an air conditioner to beat this heat," Babo said.

"If you have enough money, we have what you need!" proclaimed Ox.

Wage brought out his life savings. "Our budget is five dollars!" he said with pride.

"We're sure to have something for exactly that much!" said Wedgehead.

$1000

$100

$5

free
(act now)

As Wage and Babo happily
carried their purchase home, they heard
an odd knocking sound from inside the ice-box.
"There must be some ice in there already!" said
a very eager Wage.

When they got home, they set the ice-box down with excitement. Just then, the door popped open, revealing someone—*something*—inside!

"Hi! I'm Ice-Bat," said the frozen little fellow.

"What are you doing in our ice-box?" Wage and Babo asked.

"This is my home," said Ice-Bat with a sad little sigh.

"We're going to fill that box with cold drinks and ice!" said Wage, anxious to cool off.

When Ice-Bat flew out of the ice-box and sat on the windowsill, the entire apartment turned to ice! "WHAT DAT?!" shrieked Babo.

"Everything I touch turns to ice,"
Ice-Bat explained with a sad sigh.

"I can't play games.

I can't ride in a taxi.

I can't buy candy.

I can't eat hot soup.

I can't keep a job.

And it's really hard for me to make friends!"

Ox and Wedgehead overheard Ice-Bat and stopped in their tracks.

"Did you hear that?" said Ox. "We must get ahold of that bat! We can use him to cool off our store!"

"We'll sell ten times as many air conditioners with him around!" said Wedgehead.

"Well, what do we do now?" grumbled Ox.

"GET HIM!!!"

Ox and Wedgehead chased poor little Ice-Bat all over town.

And clear around the bend.

Past the cafe.

Around
Uglytown
Park.

By the time they passed Jeero's Gym,
Ice-Bat's wings were very tired.

"Gotcha!" said Ox.
But at that, he froze solid.
"Sorry about that," said Ice-Bat. "But everything I touch turns to ice."
Wedgehead tried to grab Ice-Bat right out of Ox's arms . . . only to become frozen himself!

The instant Ice-Bat fell to the ground, all of Uglytown turned to solid ice!

"I'm sorry!" said Ice-Bat. "I've ruined everyone's fun!"

"You didn't ruin anything!" said Wage.
"Our once hot and sticky town is a winter
wonderland," said Babo. "Thanks to you, Ice-Bat!"

And for the very first time,
Ice-Bat felt warm inside.